This book was presented to the

Bahia Vista School Library

in honor of My birthday

by Douglas Hernandez

DATE DUE

APR 1 1 1997			
K-1 P			
NOV 0 3 1997			
K-1 a			
DEC 0 1 1997			
JAN 2 6 1998			
K-3			
OCT 1 5 1998			
NOV 3 0 1998			
MAR 0 8 1999			
DEC 1 0 2007			

A Rhinoceros
Wakes Me Up in the Morning

A Bedtime Tale by Peter Goodspeed

Pictures by Dennis Panek

Bradbury Press   Scarsdale, New York

Library of Congress Cataloging in Publication Data
Goodspeed, Peter. A rhinoceros wakes me up in the morning.
Summary: A zoo of stuffed animals help a small
boy through his daily activities.
[1. Stories in rhyme.   2. Toys — Fiction]
I. Panek, Dennis, ill.   II. Title.
PZ8.3.G629Rh   [E]   81-21556
ISBN 0-87888-201-4   AACR2

Time-Life Books Inc. offers a wide range of fine
publications, including home video products. For
subscription information, call 1-800-621-7026, or write
TIME-LIFE BOOKS, P.O. Box C-32068, Richmond,
Virginia 23261-2068.

For Antonia

— P.G.

A rhinoceros wakes me up in the morning,

An elephant brushes my teeth;

A porcupine follows me down the stairs,

A panther hides underneath.

A dragon burns toast in the kitchen,

A beaver grinds oats for my gruel;

A gibbon stuffs lunch in my book bag,

A unicorn takes me to school.

Two billy goats tie up the traffic,

A crocodile cries the whole way;

A giraffe watches over the school yard,

A parrot shouts rules as we play.

A dinosaur takes names of who's talking,

A dormouse winds up the clock;

A peacock gives brushes for painting,

A packrat makes off with the chalk.

A camel drops me near home again,

A grizzly bear waits at the gate;

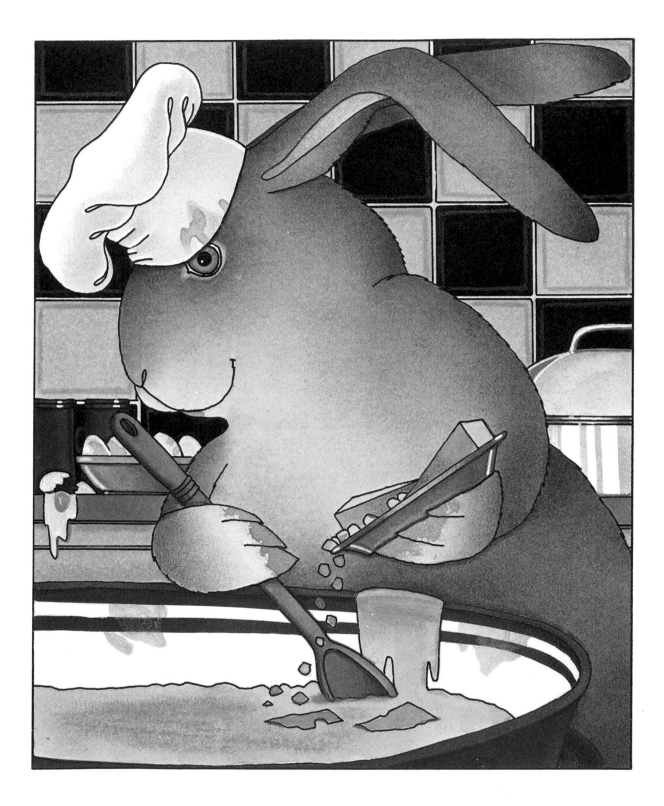

A rabbit whips up a rare cheese sauce,

A penguin skates on my plate.

A walrus draws water for bathing,

A raccoon gets lost in shampoo;

An otter sets sail in my ocean,

A hippopotamus serves as the crew.

A zebra gets my pajamas,

A panda tucks me in tight;

A toad stands guard in the doorway,

My zoo settles down for the night.